Wish Fish

Written by Sam Hay
Illustrated by Katie May
Reading Consultant: Betty Franchi

About Phonics

Spoken English uses more than 40 speech sounds. Each sound is called a *phoneme*. Some phonemes relate to a single letter (d-o-g) and others to combinations of letters (sh-ar-p). When a phoneme is written down, it is called a *grapheme*. Teaching these sounds, matching them to their written form, and sounding out words for reading is the basis of phonics.

Early phonics instruction gives children the tools to sound out, blend, and say the words without having to rely on memory or guesswork. This instruction gives children the confidence and ability to read unfamiliar words, helping them progress toward independent reading.

About the Consultant

Betty Franchi is an American educator with
a Bachelor's Degree in Elementary and Middle
Education as well as a Master's Degree in Special
Education. Betty holds a National Boards for
Professional Teaching Standards certification.
Throughout her 24 years as a teacher, she has
studied and developed an expertise in Phonetic
Awareness and has implemented phonetic strategies,
teaching many young children to read, including
students with special needs.

Reading tips

 This book focuses on the *sh* sound.

Tricky and/or new words in this book

Any words in bold may have unusual spellings
or are new and have not yet been introduced.

Tricky and/or new words in this book

**she said I of my we
was the push have**

Extra ways to have fun with this book

After the readers have finished the story, ask them
questions about what they have just read.

What does Meg find in the pond?
Why does Meg wish that she doesn't have a wish fish?

Explain that the two letters *sh* make one sound.
Think of other words that use the *sh* sound,
such as *ship* and *shop*.

I love reading.
I have lots of books
but I always wish
for more!

A Pronunciation Guide

This grid highlights the sounds used in the story and offers a guide on how to say them.

s as in sat	a as in ant	t as in tin	p as in pig	i as in ink
n as in net	c as in cat	e as in egg	h as in hen	r as in rat
m as in mug	d as in dog	g as in get	o as in ox	u as in up
l as in log	f as in fan	b as in bag	j as in jug	v as in van
w as in wet	z as in zip	y as in yet	k as in kit	qu as in quick
x as in box	ff as in off	ll as in ball	ss as in kiss	zz as in buzz
ck as in duck	pp as in puppy	nn as in bunny	rr as in arrow	gg as in egg
dd as in daddy	bb as in chubby	tt as in attic	sh as in shop	ch as in chip

Be careful not to add an /uh/ sound to /s/, /t/, /p/, /c/, /h/, /r/, /m/, /d/, /g/, /l/, /f/ and /b/. For example, say /ff/ not /fuh/ and /sss/ not /suh/.

Meg was at a pond. **She** had a net.

Tim had a ship.

"A fish!" **said** Meg.
The fish said, "**I** am a wish fish."

"Gosh!" said Meg.

"I wish I had a lot **of** cash,"
said Meg.

Pop! Meg got a shock.
"A sack of cash!" she said.

Tim held the fish. "I wish **my** ship **was** big," said Tim.

Pop! The ship was big.
But it had a bad fox on it.

"I see cash," said Fox.
Fox got off the ship.

"Stop him!" said Meg.
"Fox will rob us!"

Tim was quick. **Push**!

Fox was very wet. Fox was very mad!

"Quick!" said Tim. "Make a wish!"

"I wish I did not **have** a wish fish," said Meg.

Pop! The wish fish, cash, and Fox
are gone! The ship is not big.

Meg is sad. "**We** can get a pet fish and a big ship at a shop," says Tim.

"Yes. But not a fox!"
says Meg.

OVER 48 TITLES IN SIX LEVELS
Betty Franchi recommends...

Some titles from Level 1

Bad Rat	The Best Gift	Clint and Grant Play I-Spy	Bret and Grandma's Trip!
978 1 84898 747 0	978 1 84898 750 0	978 1 84898 752 4	978 1 84898 751 7

Other titles to enjoy from Level 2

Chuck and Duck	Let's go to the Swings	Kyle in Trouble
978 1 84898 756 2	978 1 84898 759 3	978 1 84898 762 3

Some titles from Level 3

Bart's Go-Cart	Queen Ella's Feet	Puff Flies	The Pop Duet
978 1 84898 768 5	978 1 84898 764 7	978 1 84898 765 4	978 1 84898 767 8

An Hachette Company
First Published in the United States by TickTock, an imprint of Octopus Publishing Group.
www.octopusbooksusa.com

Copyright © Octopus Publishing Group Ltd 2013

Distributed in the US by
Hachette Book Group USA
237 Park Avenue, New York NY 10017, USA

Distributed in Canada by
Canadian Manda Group
165 Dufferin Street, Toronto, Ontario, Canada M6K 3H6

ISBN 978 1 84898 755 5

Printed and bound in China
10 9 8 7 6 5 4 3 2 1